ELLIS PETERS

MONK'S · HOOD

THE MYSTERIOUS PRESS

Published by Warner Books

A Time Warner Company

If you purchase this book without a cover you should be aware that this book may have been stolen property and reported as "unsold and destroyed" to the publisher. In such case neither the author nor the publisher has received any payment for this "stripped book."

MYSTERIOUS PRESS EDITION

Copyright © 1980 by Ellis Peters
All rights reserved.

Cover design and illustration by Bascove

This Mysterious Press Edition is published by arrangement with the author.

The Mysterious Press name and logo are trademarks of Warner Books, Inc.

 Mysterious Press Books are published by
Warner Books, Inc.
1271 Avenue of the Americas
New York, NY 10020

Visit our Web site at
www.warnerbooks.com

 A Time Warner Company

Printed in the United States of America

First Mysterious Press Printing: November, 1992

15 14 13 12 11

ATTENTION: SCHOOLS AND CORPORATIONS
MYSTERIOUS PRESS books are available at quantity discounts with bulk purchase for educational, business, or sales promotional use. For information, please write to: SPECIAL SALES DEPARTMENT, MYSTERIOUS PRESS, 1271 AVENUE OF THE AMERICAS, NEW YORK, N.Y. 10020